AF405673

MOMOTARO : THE STORY OF THE SON OF A PEACH

A FAMOUS JAPANESE FAIRY TALE

GOLU KUMAR

Copyright © Golu Kumar
All Rights Reserved.

Contents

1. Chapter 1   1

ONE

An old man and an old lady lived in the distant past. They were peasants who had to work hard to get their daily rice. The elderly guy used to cut grass for the local farmers, and while he was gone, his elderly wife took care of the house chores and worked on their small rice field.

The elderly woman brought some clothing to the river to wash while the elderly man went to the hills as usual to mow the grass.

The country was stunning to see in its lush greenness as the two elderly individuals made their way to work as summer drew near. The pussy willows at the water's edge were shaking out their silky tassels, and the grass on the river's banks appeared to be emerald velvet.

The breezes blew and created wavelets on the water's clean surface. As they passed by, they brushed the old couple's cheeks, who were feeling incredibly joyful that morning for no apparent reason.

The old woman, at last, found a nice spot by the river bank and put her basket down. Then she set to work to wash the clothes; she took them one by one out of the basket and washed them in the river and rubbed them on the stones. The water was as clear as crystal, and she could see the tiny fish swimming to and fro, and the pebbles at the bottom.

A large fruit came tumbling down the stream as she was busy washing her clothes. The elderly woman noticed this big fruit when she looked up from her job.
Even though she was sixty years old, she had never before seen a peach this size.

She thought to herself, "That peach must be so good." I must undoubtedly obtain it and deliver it to my elderly father.

She extended her arm to try to grasp it, but she was unable to do so. She searched the area for a stick, but she could not find one, and if she went in search of one, she would drop the fruit.

She paused for a bit to consider what she would do and then thought of an old charm verse. Now she started clapping her hands in time with the peach rolling downstream, singing this song as she did so:

"Distant water is bitter, near water is pleasant; pass by the bitter and enter the sweet," the proverb says.

Strange to say, as soon as she began to repeat this little song the peach began to come nearer and nearer the bank where the old woman was standing, till at last, it stopped just in front of her so that she was able to take it up in her hands. The old woman was delighted. She could not go on with her work, so happy and excited was she, so she put all the clothes back in her bamboo basket, and with the basket on her back and the peach in her hand,d she hurried homewards.

She thought she had to wait a very long time for her husband to come home.
Finally, as the sun was setting, the old man returned. He had a large bundle of grass on his back, which was so large that she could hardly see him. He appeared to be quite exhausted and walked with the aid of a scythe as a walking

stick.

The elderly woman yelled out as soon as she saw him:

O,h Fii San! (Old man) I had been anticipating your return from work so eagerly today!

"What's the problem? Why are you moving so quickly? The elderly man questioned her remarkable eagerness. "Has anything occurred while I was gone?"

Oh, no, said the elderly woman, "nothing has happened; all I have done is find you a wonderful present!"

The elderly man remarked, "That is good. He then stepped up to the balcony after washing his feet in a water basin.

Now that she had entered the little space, the elderly woman retrieved the large peach from the cupboard. It was heavier than it had been. She demonstrated it to him and said:

Simply observe this! In all your life, have you ever seen a peach this size?

The elderly man was stunned when he saw the peach and exclaimed:

The biggest peach I've ever seen! Where did you purchase it?

The elderly woman responded, "I didn't buy it. "I found it while washing in the river." She then gave him the entire account.

"I am very happy you discovered it. I'm hungry, so let's eat it right away, the O Fii San stated.

When he was going to cut the peach with the kitchen knife after setting it on a board, the fruit miraculously split in half and a loud voice could be heard saying:

"Slow down, old man!" and an adorable young youngster emerged.

The elderly guy and his wife collapsed to the ground in shock at what they had seen. Once more, the youngster spoke:

"Don't be afraid. I am no demon or fairy. I will tell you the truth. Heaven has had compassion on you. Every day and every night you have lamented that you had no child. Your cry has been heard and I am sent to be the son of your old age!"

On hearing this the old man and his wife were very happy. They had cried night and day for sorrow at having no child to help them in their lonely old age, and now that their prayer was answered they were so lost with joy that they did not know where to put their hands or their feet. First,t the old man took the child up in his arms, and then the old woman did the same; and they named him MOMOTARO, OR SON OF A PEAC because he had come out of a peach.

The years passed quickly and the child grew to be fifteen years of age. He was taller and far stronger than any other boys of his age, he had a handsome face and a heart full of courage, and he was very wise for his years. The old couple's pleasure was very great when they looked at him, for he was just what they thought a hero ought to be like.

One day, Momotaro approached his foster father and sternly stated:

"Father, it's an odd coincidence that we're now father and son. Your kindness to me has beyond the mountain grasses, whose daily maintenance it was, and the river, where my mother washes the laundry. I'm at a loss for words to express my gratitude.

Why is a father's responsibility to raise his son natural? the old guy asked. There won't be any profit or loss between us since as you get older, it will be your turn to take care of us. I'm astonished that you would thank me in this manner! the elderly man,

"Why," answered the old man, "it is a matter of course that a father should bring up his son. When you are older it will be your turn to take care of us, so after all,l there will be no profit or loss between us—all will be equal. Indeed, I am rather surprised that you should thank me in this way!" and the old man looked bothered.

Momotaro stated, "I hope you'll be patient with me. But before I start repaying your kindness to me, I have a request that I hope above all else you'll grant me."

"I'll let you do whatever you want because you're not like the other males at all," the woman said.

"All right, let me leave right now."

"What say you? Do you want to leave your current parents and move away from your current house?

If you let me leave now, I'll return to you without a doubt.

Where are you headed?

"You must think it strange that I want to go away," said Momotaro, "because I have not yet told you my reason. Far away from here to the northeast of Japa,n there is an island in the sea. This island is the stronghold of a band of devils. I have often heard how they invade this land, kill and rob the people, and carry off all they can find. They are not only very wicked but they are disloyal to our Emperor and disobey his laws. They are also cannibals, for they kill and eat some of the poor people who are so unfortunate as to fall into their hands. These devils are very hateful beings. I must go and conquer them and bring back all the plunder of which they have robbed this land. It is for this reason that I want to go away for a short time!"

The old man was much surprised at hearing all this from a mere boy of fifteen. He thought it best to let the boy go. He was strong and fearless, and besides all this, the old man knew he was no common child, for he had been sent to them as a gift from Heaven, and he felt quite sure that the devils would be powerless to harm him.

"All you say is very interesting, Momotaro," said the old man. "I will not hinder you in your determination. You may go if you wish. Go to the island as soon as ever you like and destroy the demons and bring peace to the land."

Momotaro, who was getting ready to leave that day, said, "Thank you for all your kindness." He had no concept of fear because he was so courageous.

The elderly couple got to work right away, pounding rice in the kitchen mortar to produce cakes that Momotaro could take with him on his voyage.

Finally, the cakes were prepared, and Momotaro was prepared to set out on his arduous voyage.

Always sorrowful is parting. I, therefore,e became the case at this point. The two elderly people spoke while stuttering and with tears in their eyes:

"Proceed carefully and quickly. We anticipate your return, victorious.

Even though he knew he had to leave his folks behind, Momotaro was very sorry.

Momotaro was very sorry to leave his old parents (though he knew he was coming back as soon as he could), for he thought of how lonely they would be while he was away. But he said "Good-by!" quite bravely.

"I am going now. Take good care of yourselves while I am away. Good-by!" And he stepped quickly out of the house. In silence,e the eyes of Momotaro and his parents met in farewell.

Momotaro now hurried on his way till it was midday. He began to feel hungry, so he opened his bag and took out one of the rice cakes, and sat down under a tree by the side of the road to eat it. While he was thus having his lunch a dog almost as large as a colt came running out from the high grass. He made straight for Momotaro, and showing his teeth, said fiercely:

"You are a rude man to walk through my land without first getting my permission.
You may leave if you leave me all the cakes in your luggage; else, I shall bite you until you are dead.

Momotaro only mockingly laughed:

What are you saying, exactly? Do you recognize me? I'm Momotaro, and I'm headed to the northeastern Japanese island where the devils have a stronghold to conquer them. I'll cut you in half from the head down if you try to stop me on the way there.

The dog's manner at once changed. His tail dropped between his legs, and coming near he bowed so low that his forehead touched the ground.

"What do I hear? The name of Momotaro? Are you indeed Momotaro? I have often heard of your great strength. Not knowing who you were I have behaved in a very stupid way. Will you please pardon my rudeness? Are you indeed on your way to invade the Island of Devils? If you will take such a rude fellow with you as one of your followers, I shall be very grateful to you."

If you want to go, I believe I can take you with me, Momotaro said.

The dog replied, "Thank you. By the way, I'm starving to death. Can I have one of the cakes you are carrying, please?

Momotaro declared, "This is the nicest kind of cake available in Japan." I'll give you half of one because I can't spare you a complete one.

The dog took the piece that was thrown at him and said, "Thank you very much.

Then Momotaro got up and the dog followed. For a long time,e they walked over the hills and through the valleys. As they were going along an animal came down from a tree a little ahead of them. The creature soon came up to Momotaro and said:

"Momotaro, good morning! In this region of the country, you are welcome.
Will you let me accompany you?

The canine retorted enviously:

"Momotaro is already accompanied by a dog. What use are you in a fight, you monkey? We're headed there to battle the devils! Run away!

Due to their innate animosity against one another, the dog and the monkey started to fight and bite.

Now, stop arguing! Momotaro said as he stood in between them.
"Dog, hold on a second!"

The dog yelled, "It is not at all dignified for you to have such a thing following you!"

What is your knowledge of it? questioned Momotaro, who then moved the dog out of the way to address the monkey:
Identify yourself.

The monkey answered, "I am a monkey living in these hills. "I have come to join you on your journey to the Island of Devils after hearing about it. Nothing will make me happier than to acquiesce in you!"

Do you truly want to accompany me to the Island of Devils to battle there?

Yes, sir, the monkey answered.

"I applaud your bravery," Momotaro added. "This slice of one of my delicious rice cakes is here. Come in!"

So the monkey joined Momotaro. The dog and the monkey did not get on well together. They were always snapping at each other as they went along, and always wanting to fight. This made Momotaro very cross, and at last, the sent the dog on ahead with a flag and put the monkey behind with a sword, and he placed himself between them with awar fan, which is made of iron.

By and by they came to a large field. Here a bird flew down and alighted on the ground just in front of the little party. It was the most beautiful bird Momotaro had ever seen. On its body were five different robes of feathers and its head was covered with a scarlet cap.

The dog immediately charged the bird and attempted to kill it by grabbing it. However, the dog was attacked by the bird's spurs as it soared at its tail, and both engaged in a fierce struggle.

As he watched, Momotaro could not help but be impressed by the bird because it had such courage during the battle. It would undoubtedly make a capable opponent.

Momotaro approached the two combatants and said to the bird while holding the dog back:

You are silly! You make my journey more difficult. If you immediately submit, I'll take you with me. If you don't, I'll train this dog to attack you from behind.

The bird immediately gave up after that and pleaded to be taken into Momotaro's company.

"I'm not sure what justification I can make for fighting with your servant's dog, but I didn't see you. I am a pheasant, an unhappy bird. You are kind to excuse my rudeness and to take me along. I'll follow you after the dog and the monkey, please!

Momotaro grinned and added, "I commend you for submitting so quickly.

"Join us as we raid the devils. Come and join us."

The dog interrupted, "Are you going to take this bird with you also?"

"Why do you make such a pointless inquiry? Did you miss what I just said? I bring the bird along because I want to!

The dog exclaimed, "Humph!"

Momotaro then rose to his feet and ordered:

"Now all of you must listen to me. The first thing necessary in an army is harmony. It is a wise saying which says that 'Advantage on earth is better than an advantage in Heaven!' Union amongst ourselves is better than any earthly gain. When we are not at peace amongst ourselves it is no easy thing to subdue an enemy. From now, you three, the dog, the monkey,y and the pheasant must be friends with one mind. The one who first begins a quarrel will be discharged on the spot!"

Each of the threepledgede not to argue. Now included in Momotaro's suite, the pheasant was given a piece of cake.

Because of Momotaro's powerful influence, the three quickly grew close friends and followed him as their leader.

They continued moving quickly day after day until they eventually emerged onto the North Eastern Sea beach. Beyond the horizon, there was nothing to be seen and no indication of an island. The sound of waves lapping on the coast was the only thing that shattered the silence.

Now, the dog and the monkey and the pheasant had come very bravely through the long valleys and over the hills, but they had never seen the sea before, and for the first time since they set out they were bewildered and gazed at each other in silence. How were they to cross the water and get to the Island of Devils?

Soon after realizing that they were intimidated by the sight of the sea, Momotaro tried them by speaking loudly and harshly:

"Why are you holding back? Do you dread the ocean? What cowards you are, my dear! It is difficult for me to confront the demons with such frail creatures as you by my side. Going alone will be much better for me. I immediately release you all!"

The three animals clutched to Momotaro's sleeve and begged him not to send them to go after being shocked by this stern reprimand.

The dog pleaded, "Momotaro, please!"

We've gone a long way, the monkey exclaimed.

"Leaving us here is inhuman!" the pheasant stated.

The monkey said, "We are not at all afraid of the sea.

The pheasant pleaded with them to take them along.

The dog pleaded, "Do please."

Now that they had a little more courage, Momotaro said:

"Okay, then, I'll bring you along, but watch out!"

Momotaro now got a small ship, and they all got on board. The wind and weather were fair, and the ship went like an arrow over the sea. It was the first time they had ever been on the water, and so at first the dog, the monkey,y, and the pheasant were frightened at the waves and the rolling of the vessel, but by degree,s they grew accustomed to the water and were quite happy again. Every day they paced the deck of their little ship, eagerly looking out for the demons' island.

When they grew tired of this, they told each other stories of all their exploits of which they were proud, and then played games together; and Momotaro found much to amuse him in listening to the three animals and watching their antics, and in this way,y he forgot that the way was long and that he was tired of the voyage and of doing nothing. He longed to be at work killing the monsters who had done so much harm in his country.

As the wind blew in their favor and they met no storms the ship made a quick voyage, and one day when the sun was shining brightly a sight of land rewarded the four watchers at the bow.

Momotaro knew at once that what they saw was the devils' stronghold. On the top of the precipitous shore, looking out to sea, was a large castle. Now that his enterprise was close at hand, he was deep in thought with his head leaning on his hands, wondering how he should begin the attack. His three followers watched him, waiting for orders. At last, the called to the pheasant:

"It is a great advantage for us to have you with us." said Momotaro to the bird, "for you have good wings. Fly at once to the castle and engage the demons to fight. We will follow you."

The pheasant at once obeyed. He flew off from the ship beating the air gladly with his wings. The bird soon reached the island and took up his position on the roof in the middle of the castle, calling out loudly:

"All you devils listen to me! The great Japanese general Momotaro has come to fight you and to take your stronghold from you. If you wish to save your lives surrender at once, and in token of your submission you must break off the horns that grow on your forehead. If you do not surrender at once, but make up your mind to fight, we, the pheasant, the do,g, and the monkey will kill you all by biting and tearing you to death!"

Looking up and only spotting a pheasant, the horned demons laughed and said:

Indeed, a wild pheasant! Hearing such things from a cruel person like you is absurd. Wait till one of our iron bars strikes you!

Very angry, indeed, were the devils. They shook their horns and their shocks of red hair fiercely and rushed to put on tiger skin trousers to make themselves look more terrible. They then brought out great iron bars and ran to where the pheasant perched over their head and tried to knock him down. The pheasant flew to one side to escape the blow, and then attacked the head of the first one and then another demon. He flew round and round them, beating the air with his wings so fiercely and ceaselessly, that the devils began to wonder whether they had to fight one or many more birds.

In the meantime, Momotaro had brought his ship to land. As they approached, he saw that the shore was like a precipice and that the large castle was surrounded by high walls and large iron gates and was strongly fortified.

Momotaro landed, and with the hope of finding some way of entrance, walked up the path towards the top, followed by the monkey and the dog. They soon came upon two beautiful damsels washing clothes in a stream. Momotaro saw that the clothes were blood-stained and that as the two maidens washed, the tears were falling fast down their cheeks. He stopped and spoke to them:

Who are you, and what causes you to cry?

We are the Demon King's prisoners. We were taken from our homes and brought to this island, and despite being the daughters of Daimios (Lords), we are obligated to serve him. One day, he will kill us and devour us, and there will be no one to save us, the maidens said, holding up the blood-stained clothing.

And at this awful notion, more tears began to fall from their eyes.

Momotaro promised to save him. Please only show me how I can enter the castle; do not cry any longer.

The two women then led the way and showed Momotaro a little back entrance that was so small that he could almost go through it at the lowest part of the castle wall.

The pheasant, who had been engaged in a fierce battle, watched Momotaro and his small group come in from behind.

Momotaro's onslaught was so furious that the devils could not stand against him. At first, their foe had been a single bird, the pheasant, but now that Momotaro and the dog and the monkey had arrived they were bewildered, for the four enemies fought like a hundred, so strong were they. Some of the devils fell off the parapet of the castle and were dashed to pieces on the rocks beneath; others fell into the sea and were drowned; many were beaten to death by the three animals.

Finally, the sole remaining devil was the chief. He made up his resolve to give up since he understood that his adversary was more powerful than a mere man.

He approached Momotaro with humility, threw down his iron staff, and then, bowing before the victor, broke off the horns on his head as a show of submission because they were a representation of his might and dominance.

He said softly, "I'm terrified of you. "I am unable to oppose you. If you will spare my life, I will give you every piece of riches buried inside this fortress.

Momotaro chuckled.

"Big Devil, pleading for pity is not typical of you, is it? Despite your pleading, I cannot spare your wicked life because you have long been robbing our nation and killing and torturing many people.

The devil leader was then bound and subjected to the monkey's charge by Momotaro. After accomplishing this, he entered every room of the castle, released the inmates, and collected all the valuables he discovered.

The loot was brought home by the dog and the pheasant, and Momotaro joyfully made his way back to his house while holding the devil leader hostage.

The two pitiful damsels, daughters of Daimios, as well as the other slaves that the evil demon had abducted, were taken in safety to their own homes and handed over to their parents.

On his triumphant return, Momotaro was hailed as a hero by the entire nation, which also celebrated the nation's liberation from the long-standing menace of the robber devils.

The old couple was happier than ever, and thanks to the treasure Momotaro had brought home with him, they could live out their days in comfort and abundance.

www.ingramcontent.com/pod-product-compliance
Lightning Source LLC
Chambersburg PA
CBHW061412160726
47995CB00002B/576